The Little Engine That Could™

Saves the Thanksgiving Day Parade!

Platt & Munk, Publishers

To J.C.—C.O.

Library of Congress Cataloging-in-Publication Data

Piper, Watty, pseud.
  The little engine that could saves the Thanksgiving Day parade / by Watty Piper ; illustrated by Cristina Ong.
      p. cm.
Summary: The Turkeyland Band is on its way to play in Gobbleville's Thanksgiving Day parade when a tire goes flat and they have no spare, but the Little Blue Engine comes by and thinks she can help.
 [1. Railroads--Trains--Fiction. 2. Bands (Music)--Fiction. 3. Parades--Fiction. 4. Thanksgiving Day--Fiction.] I. Ong, Cristina, ill. II. Title.
  PZ7.P64 Lp 2002
  [E]--dc21
                          2002004763

ISBN 0-448-42861-X   A B C D E F G H I J

The Little Engine That Could™

Saves the Thanksgiving Day Parade!

by Watty Piper
illustrated by Cristina Ong

Platt & Munk, Publishers

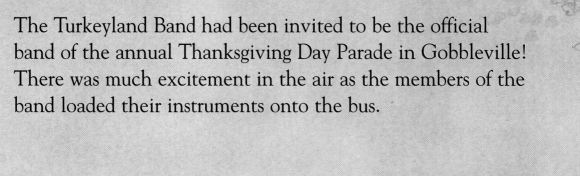

The Turkeyland Band had been invited to be the official band of the annual Thanksgiving Day Parade in Gobbleville! There was much excitement in the air as the members of the band loaded their instruments onto the bus.

It was a cool, crisp fall day. The bus carrying the band bumped along the road.

The sounds of the tuning of the tuba, the crashing of the cymbals, and the high-pitched trilling of the flute floated out of the half-opened windows.

The bus stopped for a red light at the train
tracks. When the light turned green, the bus
started to move. But just as it crossed the train
tracks there was a loud *pop*! The bus stopped.

The bus driver was worried. He got out of the
bus to see what had happened. Big John went
with the driver to check out the problem.

When Big John climbed back on the bus, his face looked sad. "I'm afraid I have some bad news," he told the rest of the band. "The bus has a flat and there is no spare tire!"

Oh, no! How would the Turkeyland
Band get to Gobbleville now?

"Maybe we can catch a ride," said Susie Cranberry, the flute player. But there was no one else on the road.

"Can we walk there?" asked Little Tim, who played the cymbals and was the youngest member of the band.

"I wish we could," said Big John,
"but it's much too far to walk."

Just then, the Little Blue Engine came chugging happily down the track. "What seems to be the problem?" she asked in a sweet little voice.

"We have a flat tire and no spare to change it with," said the bus driver.

"We're supposed to play in Gobbleville's Thanksgiving parade," Susie Cranberry added. "But we'll never get there in time now!" She wiped a tear from her cheek.

"I'm not very fast, but I think I can get you to Gobbleville in time for the parade. I think I can," said the Little Blue Engine.

"We'll unload the bus as fast as we can," said Big John.

"I'll help too," said the jolly clown, the Little Blue Engine's best friend.

When she was all loaded, the Little Blue Engine tried to move. *Chugga*—stop. *Chugga, chugga*—stop. With the Turkeyland Band and all their instruments, her load was so heavy! But the little engine said to herself—I think I can—I think I can—and soon she began to move.

Puff, puff, chug, chug—the Little Blue Engine moved steadily down the tracks. Before long, she came to a hill. And on the other side of the hill was Gobbleville! But it was such a big, big hill and the Little Blue Engine was so tired. Yet she wasn't going to let that stop her.

She looked at the hill and repeated to herself—I think I can—I think I can. "We know you can, we know you can," the band members chanted. And the Little Blue Engine puffed and chugged all the way up the hill and then all the way down to the other side.

With the Little Blue Engine's help, the Turkeyland Band made it to Gobbleville just in time for the parade!

Happy Thanksgiving

The whole town greeted the band and the Little Blue Engine as they pulled into sight. "Hip, hip, hooray for Little Blue," Susie Cranberry yelled. Everyone cheered.

The Gobbleville Thanksgiving Day Parade began. The Little Blue Engine was asked to follow the track down Stuffington Street as the band marched along the parade route. The jolly clown did cartwheels and handstands alongside the band as they made their way down the street.

When the parade was over, the jolly clown hopped back aboard the Little Blue Engine. The bus driver and the entire Turkeyland Band came over to say thank you and good-bye.

The Little Blue Engine pulled away as the band sat down to a much deserved Thanksgiving feast.